Uncle Willy's Tickles

A CHILD'S RIGHT
TO SAY NO

Second Edition

For my beloved family — MA

Published by
MAGINATION PRESS
An Educational Publishing Foundation Book
American Psychological Association
750 First Street, NE
Washington, DC 20002

For more information about our books, including a complete catalog, please write to us,
call 1-800-374-2721, or visit our website at www.maginationpress.com.

The text type is Wilke Roman.
Printed by Phoenix Color, Rockaway, New Jersey

Library of Congress Cataloging-in-Publication Data

Aboff, Marcie.
Uncle Willy's tickles : a child's right to say no / written by Marcie Aboff ;
illustrated by Kathleen Gartner.— 2nd ed.
p. cm.
Summary: Uncle Willy will not stop tickling, even when his nephew says "stop,"
but with reassurance from his mother the boy tries again to tell Uncle Willy he tickles
too much. Includes a note to parents on how to talk about "good and bad touching"
and a child's right to say no.
ISBN 1-55798-998-2 (hardcover : alk. paper) — ISBN 1-55798-999-0 (pbk. : alk. paper)
[1. Uncles—Fiction. 2. Tickling—Fiction. 3. Children's rights—Fiction.]
I. Gartner, Kathleen, ill. II. Title.
PZ7.A164Uo 2003
[E]—dc21   2002152689

Manufactured in the United States of America
10 9 8 7 6 5 4 3 2 1

Uncle Willy's Tickles

A CHILD'S RIGHT
TO SAY NO

Second Edition

written by Marcie Aboff
illustrated by Kathleen Gartner

MAGINATION PRESS • WASHINGTON, DC

When Uncle Willy comes to visit, he lets me sit behind the wheel of his new blue pickup truck. I'm higher than all the cars on the street.

When Uncle Willy comes to visit, he takes me and
my sister Carly to Ice Cream Haven for my favorite
chocolate chip, double scoop, hot fudge-and-whipped-
cream sundae. With rainbow sprinkles, too.

When Uncle Willy comes to visit,
Mom and Dad laugh at his jokes.

Uncle Willy can wiggle his ears
without even touching them.

And he can run backward without even banging into a wall.

I laugh and laugh and laugh.

When Uncle Willy comes to visit, he likes to tickle me. He tickles me under my chin, under my arms, on top of my head, just about everywhere! It makes me laugh at first, but sometimes Uncle Willy keeps tickling me… and tickling me… and tickling me.

"Stop, stop," I say.

But sometimes Uncle Willy keeps tickling me until my sides ache and my insides feel like splitting apart.

My sister Carly says Uncle Willy
tickles all the kids. She thinks it's
funny. But I still don't like the
way he keeps tickling me.

Uncle Willy is coming for dinner tonight.
If he tickles me, I'll run to my room.

I'll paint my skin with red dots and say
I have the chicken pox and can't come out.

Maybe I'll disguise myself
as a pirate captain.
No one will recognize me.

Maybe I'll hide underneath the table. Uncle Willy will be so busy eating spaghetti that he won't even notice me.

18

Knock. Knock.

"Kyle," my mother calls. "Uncle Willy is here. We'll be eating in ten minutes."

"I'm not hungry," I say.

Mom comes into my room. She puts her hand on my forehead. She always does that when I tell her I'm not hungry for dinner.

"You don't have a fever," she says. "Do you feel sick?"

I don't want to tell her about Uncle Willy's tickles. She'll probably say Uncle Willy tickles all the kids.

But I tell her anyway. Mom is quiet for a little while. Then she says, "You did the right thing by telling me. Did you tell Uncle Willy you don't like the way he tickles you?"

"Sometimes I tell him to stop, but he keeps tickling me anyway."

Mom says, "Uncle Willy shouldn't keep tickling you when you tell him to stop. Your body belongs to you. No one has a right to tickle you or touch you in a way you don't like. Let's go tell him again tonight."

Mom hugs me. I tell her I'm getting hungry for dinner.

When I walk downstairs, I see Dad and
Uncle Willy talking. Uncle Willy looks up
at me and smiles. I smile back.

"Hey buddy," Uncle Willy says. I jump down
the bottom step and Uncle Willy pats my back.
Then he starts tickling me around my neck.

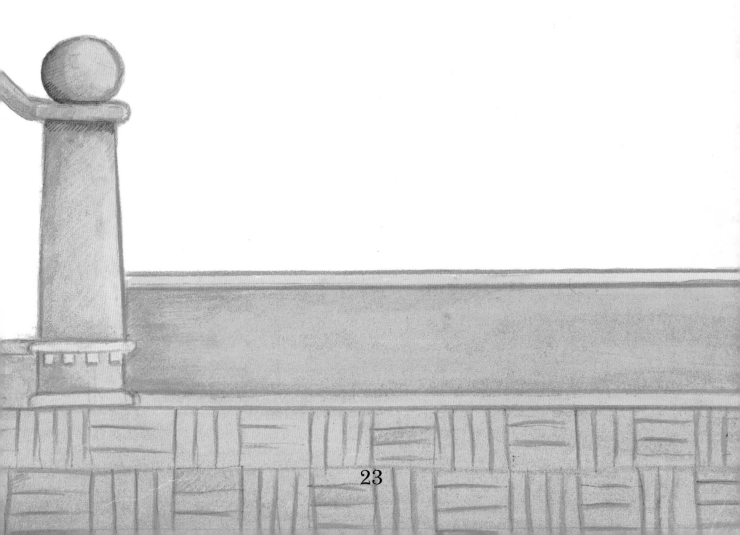

I pull away. "NO!" I say.
"You tickle me too much
and I don't like it."

Uncle Willy steps back.
"Hey! No problem,"
he says.

After dinner, Uncle Willy asks if I want to play checkers in the den. As I move my black checker toward his red checker, he says, "I'm glad you told me you don't like the way I tickle you." I look down at the checkerboard and nod.

"And you can be sure I won't do it anymore."

I look up and Uncle Willy holds his hand in the air. "Give me a high-five," he says. I high-five Uncle Willy as hard as I can.

Uncle Willy rolls over backward and kicks his feet in the air!

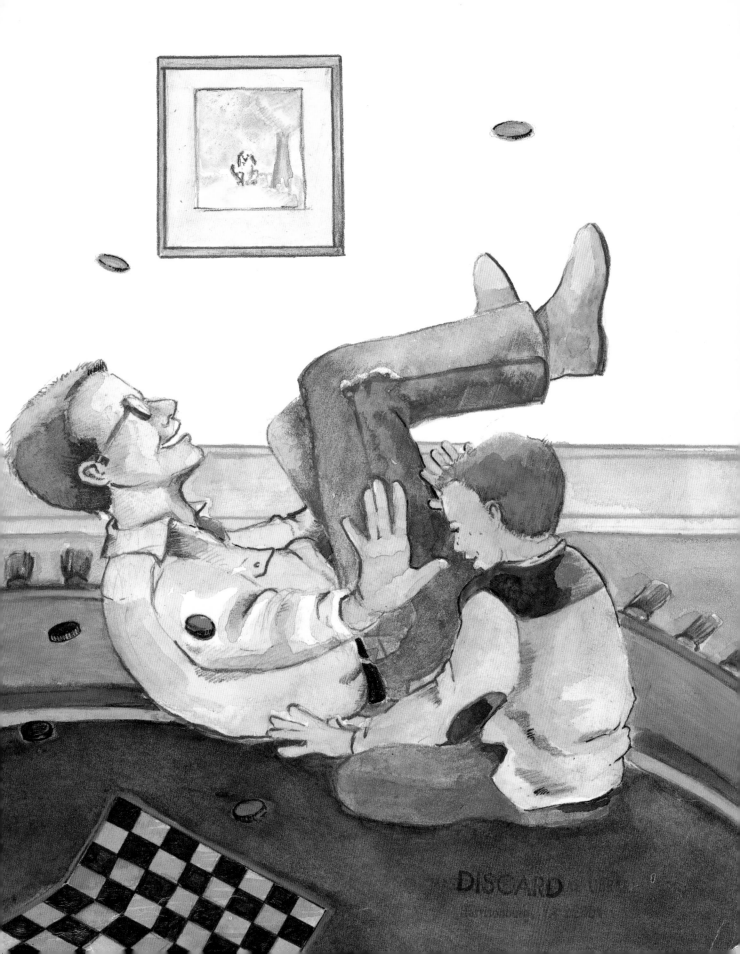

He shakes out his hand and grins. "Whoooa," Uncle Willy says with a big smile. "You are one strong kid!"

I laugh and laugh and laugh.

I like my Uncle Willy.

Note to Parents

BY JANE ANNUNZIATA, PSY.D.

Physical expressions of affection contribute substantially to a healthy emotional life. But *Uncle Willy's Tickles* shows how physical contact that seems harmless can cause problems for kids. The book also offers parents a non-threatening story line for teaching children about the privacy of their bodies and their right to say no to any kind of uncomfortable touch.

FROM THE CHILD'S PERSPECTIVE

Physical Discomfort. Tickling and other unwanted or inappropriate touches are physically uncomfortable. A few seconds of tickling once in awhile can be manageable for some children, but many can't tolerate it at all. This should be respected.

Emotional Discomfort. Tickling makes kids feel helpless and out of control. Children can also feel overwhelmed by the physical sensation of tickling (especially when it is excessive and/or frequent) and desperate to avoid it. Feelings of desperation and loss of control are exacerbated when the child says "stop" but the request is ignored.

Feelings of Anger. Tickling makes children feel angry because it is overstimulating and out of their control. They feel especially angry when their requests for it to stop go unheard, or when others find it funny.

Feelings of Violation and Disrespect. Tickling leaves children feeling violated and disrespected. It is intrusive and a violation of one's body or personal space. It also goes against everything we try to teach children about their bodies being private.

Control Issues. Excessive tickling can contribute to the development of control issues. This occurs because the child is trying to find a way to manage or discharge the out-of-control feelings. Children may become controlling themselves to try to compensate. Parents may not always see or make this connection, but it can be there.

Damaged Relationships. Tickling interferes with what otherwise could be a rewarding relationship for the child. If the tickling is allowed to occur or continue, the child may withdraw from the person as a way to cope, as Kyle does in this story.

FOR PARENTS TO REMEMBER

Consistent Messages. Parents work hard to teach children about good and bad touches and saying no when someone does something that makes them uncomfortable. Allowing tickling to occur goes against this message.

Clear Statements About Rights. "Your body belongs to you. No one has a right to tickle you or touch you in a way you don't like," says Kyle's mother. Such clear statements from parents help kids internalize this message and increase the likelihood that children can say no when something makes them uncomfortable.

Age-Appropriate Intervention. Parents' steps to help stop undesired physical behavior need to be age-appropriate. Kyle's mother joins with her child by saying, "*Let's* go tell him again tonight." Trying to empower the child to stand up for him- or herself is fine, but the added boost from a parent is often needed. Also, it says to the child, "I take this very seriously. We will make sure that it ends."

Parental Awareness. Parents need to intervene whether or not the child is able to come forward and say it's an issue. Kyle is able to let his mom know something is bothering him, but not all kids can. Therefore, parents need to be aware of the discomfort children feel in these situations and stop them, even if the child minimizes the distress or can't directly show it.

Uncomfortable Confrontations. Parents need to protect children, even if it puts the parent in an awkward position vis-a-vis a relative or an adult friend. When parents come forward, the child benefits enormously and feels great relief; when they don't, children resent them.

Resistance and Minimizing. Parents must not be deterred by comments made by the tickler such as, "You're exaggerating, tickling is just harmless fun." Unwanted touches are not "just fun" and need to be stopped.

Child's Right to Control. Parents need to follow the child's lead regarding what feels good/comfortable and bad/intrusive. In most other areas (e.g., discipline, determining chores, etc.), parents should exercise control. But children should have control over their bodies and what does or doesn't feel good.

Tickling Among Peers. Tickling can be problematic even when it occurs between siblings or same-age friends, for all the reasons detailed above.

Other Physical Behaviors. Other behaviors that may also seem innocent can be as troublesome as tickling. These include wrestling, especially when it occurs between parents and kids, or between opposite-sex friends, or when it is unwanted by one of the parties. Behaviors such as wrestling are concerning for all the reasons described above and because they can quickly become aggressive and overstimulating for children. In general, any physical behavior that causes a child to feel uncomfortable and intruded upon (excessive or age-inappropriate affection, body touches in particularly private parts of the body, tickling, wrestling, etc.) should be avoided.

Dr. Annunziata is an author and clinical psychologist with a private practice for children and families in McLean, Virginia.